KT-478-697

For
Michael John

J.C.

For
Mum and Dad

S.L.

First published 1993 by
Walker Books Ltd
87 Vauxhall Walk
London SE11 5HJ

This edition published 1995

8 10 9

Text © 1993 June Crebbin
Illustrations © 1993 Stephen Lambert

This book has been typeset in Goudy.

Printed in Hong Kong

British Library Cataloguing in Publication Data
A catalogue record for this book is
available from the British Library.

ISBN 0-7445-3627-8

FLY BY NIGHT

Written by June Crebbin

Illustrated by Stephen Lambert

WALKER BOOKS
AND SUBSIDIARIES
LONDON • BOSTON • SYDNEY

Once, at the edge of a wood, lived two owls, a mother owl and her young one, Blink. Every day, all day long, they slept. Every night, all night long, the mother owl flew and Blink waited.

One day,
when the sun
was still low in the sky, Blink opened
one eye and said, "Now? Is it time?"
"Soon," said his mother. "Soon.
Go back to sleep."

Blink tried
to sleep.

When the sun rose and warmed the earth,
he opened the other eye. "*Now* is it time?"
"Not yet," said his mother. "Soon.
Go back to sleep."

Blink tried.

Butterflies looped and drifted
past him. Beetles scuttled in the
undergrowth. Near by, a
woodpecker tapped on
a tree trunk.

Blink couldn't sit still.

"Is it time *yet?*" he said.

His mother opened her eyes.

"You are old enough and strong

enough –" Blink dithered with

excitement – "but you must wait."

His mother closed her eyes.

The sun was at its highest.
A squirrel leapt from tree to
tree, quicker than a thought.
Along Blink's branch it came,
right past him, its tail
streaming out behind.
Blink wriggled and jiggled.
He *couldn't* sit still.

 All that long afternoon,
he watched and
waited. He shuffled and fidgeted.
Below, in the clearing, a deer and
its fawn browsed on leaves and twigs.
High above, a kestrel hovered, dipped
and soared again into the sky.
"When will it be *my* time?" said
Blink to himself.

Towards dusk, a sudden gust
of wind, sweeping through
the wood, lifting leaves on
their branches, seemed to
gather Blink from his branch
as if it would lift him too.
"Time to fly," it seemed to say.
Blink fluffed out his feathers.
He shifted his wings.

But the wind swirled by.

It was all puff and nonsense.

Blink sighed. He closed his eyes.

The sun slipped behind the fields.

The moon rose pale and clear.

A night breeze stirred. "Time to fly."

"Puff and nonsense," muttered Blink.

"*Time to fly*," said his mother beside him.

Blink sat up. "Is it?"

he said. "Is it? *Really?*"

The grey dusk had deepened.

Blink heard soft whisperings.

He saw the stars in the sky.

He felt the dampness of the

night air. He knew it was

time to fly. He gathered his

strength. He drew himself up.

He stretched out his wings and –

lifted into the air.

Higher and higher.

He flew. Further and further.

Over the wood, over the fields,

over the road and the sleeping city.

High in the sky, his wing-beats strong,

Blink flew on over the sleeping city –
and over the fields and the winding river.

His first flight; a fly-by-night.

MORE WALKER PAPERBACKS
For You to Enjoy

THE CATS OF TIFFANY STREET
by Sarah Hayes

Every Friday night, six cats meet and dance at the end of Tiffany Street.
Then along comes the man with a van and takes them away.

"Admirably suited to reading aloud … will give great pleasure. The pictures are bold,
colourful and full of movement and witty detail. The story is a good one too."
The Times Educational Supplement

0-7445-3162-4   £4.99

WHAT IS THE SUN?
by Reeve Lindbergh/Stephen Lambert

"A book of lasting distinction. Neatly skilled, simple verse, allied perfectly
to Stephen Lambert's sensitive artwork, captures with quiet, accurate humour the relentless
questioning adults undergo from children. There is also much to be learned here
about the natural world." *Books for Keeps*

0-7445-4312-6   £4.99

OWL BABIES
by Martin Waddell/Patrick Benson

On a tree in the woods, three baby owls, Sarah and Percy and Bill, wait
for their Owl Mother to come home in this bedtime story by the author of
Can't You Sleep, Little Bear? and the illustrator of *The Minipins*.

"Touchingly beautiful… Drawn with exquisite delicacy… The perfect picture book."
The Guardian

0-7445-3167-5   £4.99

Walker Paperbacks are available from most booksellers, or by post from B.B.C.S., P.O. Box 941, Hull, North Humberside HU1 3YQ
24 hour telephone credit card line 01482 224626

To order, send: Title, author, ISBN number and price for each book ordered, your full name and address,
cheque or postal order payable to BBCS for the total amount and allow the following for postage and packing:
UK and BFPO: £1.00 for the first book, and 50p for each additional book to a maximum of £3.50.
Overseas and Eire: £2.00 for the first book, £1.00 for the second and 50p for each additional book.

Prices and availability are subject to change without notice.

THIS WALKER BOOK BELONGS TO:

(Miss Archer)

St Vincent's School W3

LIBRARY

"C"
green Let
1F
gold star